Doggy Drama

Doggy Drama

Lucy Daniels

With special thanks to Caryn Jenner
To Lia Leonard, who wants to be a vet

ORCHARD BOOKS

First published in Great Britain in 2019 by The Watts Publishing Group

1 3 5 7 9 10 8 6 4 2

Text copyright © Working Partners Ltd, 2019
Illustrations copyright © Working Partners Ltd, 2019

A CIP catalogue record for this book
is available from the British Library.

ISBN 978 1 40835 406 3

Printed and bound in Great Britain by CPI Group (UK) Ltd, Croydon, CR0 4YY

The paper and board used in this book are made from wood from responsible sources.

Orchard Books
An imprint of
Hachette Children's Group
Part of The Watts Publishing Group Limited
Carmelite House
50 Victoria Embankment
London EC4Y 0DZ

An Hachette UK Company
www.hachette.co.uk
www.hachettechildrens.co.uk

CONTENTS

CHAPTER ONE

Amelia Haywood beamed with pride as she gazed at the sign by the door of the stone cottage: ANIMAL ARK, VETERINARY SURGERY.

My dream has come true!

Ever since she'd moved to the village of Welford a few months ago, she'd wanted to help out at Animal Ark. At first Mr and Mrs Hope, the vets who owned the surgery, had thought that Amelia was too young. But she and her friend Sam had proved that they were up to the job. Now they were officially helping out at Animal Ark on weekends and some mornings before school.

"Am I late?"

Amelia turned to see Sam round the bend in the lane and run up to her, his school backpack on his shoulder. "You don't need to rush – we're early," she called to him.

"I couldn't get away," Sam said, gasping for breath. "Mac kept trying to follow me."

Mac was Sam's cute Westie puppy.

"Maybe he was upset that he couldn't come with you," Amelia said, laughing. "But we've got too many other animals to look after this morning."

"You certainly do!" It was Mrs Hope, her red hair bobbing as she climbed the steps behind them. She unlocked the door and let Amelia and Sam into the empty waiting room, while Mr Hope parked their car.

"What should we do first?" asked Amelia eagerly.

Mrs Hope smiled. "You can start by looking after the animals in the hotel."

The hotel was what the Hopes called the overnight stay area. It was where

Star had stayed with her mum and the other kittens after they were born. Amelia and Sam had fed the kittens and played with them. Now Star was Amelia's very own pet!

Julia Kaminski, the receptionist, arrived next, propelling her wheelchair up the ramp behind Mr Hope. "Hello, you two!" She smiled at Amelia and Sam as she turned on the computer at the reception desk.

"I'll start getting ready for today's appointments," said Mrs Hope. "Would you check the emails, Julia?" she asked the receptionist. "Let me know if there's anything urgent."

"Of course," Julia replied.

Mrs Hope went into her office while Amelia and Sam followed Mr Hope down the corridor, past the examination rooms to the hotel. As they entered the overnight room, a strange, high-pitched voice called out, "What a naughty boy! What a naughty boy!"

Startled, Sam jumped. "Who said that?"

Amelia laughed when she realised

that the voice came from a bright green parrot in a large birdcage. She peered inside for a closer look and saw a dressing around one of the parrot's wings.

"Meet Gabby," said Mr Hope. "She flew into a window and broke her wing." Next he pointed to a grey rabbit sleeping on a pile of straw, a bandage across his middle.

"Hoppy had surgery to remove a tumour in his stomach. And Clementine has an infected foot," he finished, pointing to a tortoise in a tank.

"Poor things," said Sam.

"They're all on the road to recovery," said Mr Hope. "It will just take time."

While Mr Hope checked the animals' wounds, Amelia and Sam cleaned out the pens.

"Gross," said Sam, wiping gooey bird droppings out of Gabby's cage.

"Gross!" the parrot repeated.

Amelia laughed. She had to agree. *But it's worth it to be around these animals!* She cleaned out Hoppy's rabbit droppings, then lined the hutch with fresh paper and straw.

"Great job," said Mr Hope when they had finished.

Amelia grinned at Sam as they washed their hands in the sink. Then Mr Hope led them back down the corridor to the reception area. There, a black and white sheepdog sat at the feet of a farmer with a bushy grey beard. The dog's chin rested on the man's Wellington boot.

"Good morning, Mr Nicholls," said Mr Hope. "What's the matter with Lucy?"

"She's off her food," the farmer replied, looking worried. "I think she might have a tummy ache."

Mr Hope knelt down and gently opened the dog's mouth. Plucking a small torch from his shirt pocket, he peered inside. The dog whined.

"Poor creature," whispered Amelia. "Her belly must really hurt!"

"It's not her tummy – it's her tooth," said Mr Hope. "It will need to be taken out, I'm afraid. We'll do it this morning and you can collect Lucy in the afternoon."

Mr Nicholls stroked the dog's head. The vet led the way to the treatment room, calling for Lucy to follow, but she stayed loyally by the farmer's side.

"Go with Mr Hope, Lucy," Mr Nicholls said. "I'll see you this afternoon."

The clever sheepdog looked back at her owner, then trotted into the treatment room.

"Mr Hope will take good care of her," Amelia assured the farmer.

"I know," said Mr Nicholls. "I hope we find a vet as nice as him in our new town."

"You're moving?" said Sam.

Mr Nicholls nodded. "I've retired and sold all of my animals apart from Lucy and my two llamas."

"Llamas? In Welford?" Amelia said, surprised. She was always discovering new things in the countryside!

"Yes, but I need to find them a new home," Mr Nicholls said.

"You can put a sign up here." Amelia pointed to the notice board that covered a wall in the reception area. There were lots of posters giving advice to pet owners, but also a section about missing animals and pets needing new homes. "Sam and I will help, too."

"We found homes for four kittens,"

Sam told the farmer proudly.

"Llamas are a lot bigger than kittens. Do you really think you could find someone to adopt them?" Mr Nicholls asked doubtfully.

Amelia grinned at Sam, and he grinned back.

"We'll give it a shot!" said Amelia.

CHAPTER TWO

As Mr Nicholls left the surgery, he held the door for a young woman with short hair tucked behind her ears. She was carrying an animal wrapped in a blanket. A furry brown tail poked out through the folds.

"Hi, Miss Sachs!" said Sam.

Amelia realised it was their drama club teacher from school. Tucked in the blanket, a cute little brown Yorkshire terrier gazed at them with big eyes. A cast covered one of his front legs.

"Oh no!" said Amelia. "What happened?"

"He was trying to swim," said Miss Sachs. She sighed and rubbed the puppy's ears. "Oscar can't resist playing in the water. He jumped into a river but the water was too shallow. His leg broke when he hit the bottom. Luckily, he's having his cast taken off today."

Mrs Hope called Miss Sachs and Oscar into the treatment room. "You two can come and help," she said to Amelia and Sam.

They shared an excited smile, and followed Miss Sachs and the patient. In the treatment room, Mrs Hope lifted Oscar on to the examining table. Sam stroked him gently to keep him calm, while Amelia held his leg still for Mrs Hope. Carefully, the vet cut the cast off with a large pair of scissors. Oscar

yawned and licked his lips nervously,
but he didn't flinch.

What a good dog, thought Amelia.

Mrs Hope unwrapped the bandage
and padding that was underneath the
cast, then felt along Oscar's leg. Amelia
watched intently.

"It feels like the break has healed,"
said Mrs Hope. "What do you think,
little guy? Do you want to try walking
on it?"

Gently, she put Oscar on the floor.
Amelia held her breath.

Oscar lifted his bad leg off the floor
and hobbled along on his three good
legs. He stopped and his tail drooped.

"Go on, Oscar,"
Miss Sachs
encouraged him.

But the dog just
lay down at her
feet. He sniffed at
his newly exposed
leg and licked the fur.

"Poor Oscar," said Amelia. "He's not
feeling very playful."

"I guess he's not ready to put any
weight on it yet," said Mrs Hope. "It
will take some time for him to get back
to normal. In the meantime, he'll need
some light exercise, along with lots of
extra love and attention."

"Oh dear." Miss Sachs frowned. "The school play is coming up and I haven't got much time right now."

Amelia exchanged a glance with Sam. Last week they'd auditioned for parts in the school play, but with all the excitement of becoming a helper at Animal Ark, Amelia had forgotten about it.

"My usual dog walker takes Oscar out with a group of dogs, so he can't give Oscar any extra attention," Miss Sachs continued. "What am I going to do?"

Amelia leaned over and stroked Oscar's smooth, silky fur. "I wish there was something I could do to help," she murmured, as the dog nuzzled her hand with his soft, warm nose.

"Me too!" added Sam.

Miss Sachs wrapped the dog up in the blanket again and carried him to the door. "I'll see you two at drama club," she called to Amelia and Sam.

After Miss Sachs and Oscar had left, Mrs Hope said, "So you two are budding actors as well as vets."

"We're doing *The Wizard of Oz*," Sam told her. "I want to be the Tin Man."

"I auditioned to be Dorothy," said Amelia.

"And is Mac going to be Dorothy's dog, Toto?" asked Mrs Hope.

"I hope so!" said Sam. "He'd be great on stage. He's really well behaved now." He grinned and added, "Most of the time, anyway."

Talking about the play reminded Amelia that they still had a whole day of school ahead of them. She looked at the clock. "Sam, we'd better go or we'll be late!"

"Well, thanks for all your help!" said Mrs Hope. "See you again tomorrow morning!"

"Obviously Miss Sachs will pick me to be Dorothy," Tiffany declared after school. "I'm going to be a famous actress when I grow up."

Sam rolled his eyes and Amelia stifled a giggle at their classmate's boasting. The drama club was in the classroom, waiting for Miss Sachs to come and announce the cast for *The Wizard of Oz*.

"And Sparkle will make the perfect Toto," Tiffany continued. "He's so clever. He can roll over, sit up and beg, and even fetch my headphones." Sparkle was Tiffany's Bichon Frise – a fluffy white puppy, who she usually carried around in a special backpack.

Just then, Miss Sachs arrived, followed by Oscar on his lead. The tiny terrier was still hobbling on three legs.

Amelia knelt down next to him. "Hello, Oscar. Remember me?"

Oscar's tail wagged as he licked her hand. *If only I could help you get better …* thought Amelia.

"Gather round, everyone," said Miss Sachs. She held up a clipboard. "I've got the cast list here."

Immediately, everyone was quiet. Amelia's heart beat faster.

"I'm afraid you can't all have the

part you want," Miss Sachs continued. "Otherwise, we'd have seven Dorothys! But you're all important to the success of the play, no matter which role you have."

She looked at her list. "The role of the Cowardly Lion goes to Caleb. Karel, I've chosen you to be the Tin Man."

Amelia glanced over at Sam. He looked disappointed.

"Sam, I think you'll make an excellent Scarecrow," said Miss Sachs.

"Cool!" Sam's face immediately lit up, his brown eyes sparkling.

"Izzy, you've got the part of Glinda the Good Witch," Miss Sachs went on.

Amelia saw her friend clap her hands with glee.

"And Tiffany," said Miss Sachs, "with your dramatic talent, I think you'll be perfect for—"

"Dorothy!" Tiffany shouted. "I'm Dorothy!"

"Actually," said Miss Sachs, "you're

going to be the Wicked
Witch of the West."

"But who's playing
Dorothy?" wailed
Tiffany.

Miss Sachs looked at
her clipboard. "Well,
I had a tough choice,
especially as so many of you tried out
to be Dorothy. But I've decided to cast
Amelia because she did such a great
audition."

Me? Amelia wasn't sure she'd heard
correctly.

"Well done, Amelia!" said Sam.

Amelia blushed, especially when her

friends gathered round to congratulate her. But she spotted Tiffany glaring at her from the other side of the room.

"Miss Sachs, who's going to be Toto?" asked Sam.

Miss Sachs smiled. "Well, I've heard your dog Mac is very well trained, so it makes sense for him to take the role. Toto is supposed to be a terrier, after all."

Everyone erupted into cheers – except for Tiffany, who was dabbing her eyes with a tissue.

Even though Tiffany wasn't very nice, Amelia was sorry to see her upset. She took a deep breath and walked over to her. "The Wicked Witch is actually a really good part, Tiffany."

"No, it's not." Tiffany scowled at her.

"You can have loads of fun cackling and casting spells," Amelia went on. "The Wicked Witch is the *real* star of the play."

Tiffany sniffed. "Do you really think so?"

"Of course. And like Miss Sachs said, you'll be brilliant at it."

Tiffany sniffed again and smiled.

"I will, won't I?" she said.

"Listen up," called Miss Sachs, passing round copies of the script. "Please learn the opening scene for tomorrow's rehearsal. Good luck, everyone!"

CHAPTER THREE

After drama club, Amelia and Sam walked to his house, the Old Mill Bed and Breakfast. She couldn't quite believe she'd been cast in the main part, and it filled her with a mixture of excitement and dread.

I hope I don't let Miss Sachs down...

"I can't wait to tell Mac that he's going to play Toto!" exclaimed Sam.

Mr Baxter, Sam's dad, was in the kitchen baking scones for the B&B guests. His dark hair was speckled with flour. "Hi, guys! How was school today?"

"Brilliant!" Sam replied. "Guess what, Dad? I'm playing the Scarecrow in the school play!"

"Congratulations!" Mr Baxter gave Sam a high five.

"And Amelia's Dorothy. Isn't that great? And Mac is Toto!" Sam grabbed a packet of cocktail sausages from the fridge. "Come on, let's go and find him."

Sam and Amelia caught sight of the little white puppy in the lounge. He was stretched out on the sofa next to Mr Ferguson, who often stayed at the B&B when he had business meetings nearby. From the doorway, they could see Mr Ferguson stroking Mac.

"Who's a cutie wootie?" Mr Ferguson was saying in a funny voice.

"I thought Mr Ferguson didn't like Mac," Amelia whispered.

"He doesn't," Sam whispered back. "At least, that's what he says."

Amelia followed him into the lounge. Startled, Mr Ferguson quickly pulled his hand away. His face settled into its usual grumpy scowl. "Er … I was just checking the dog for fleas."

Mr Ferguson picked up his motorbike helmet and stomped out of the room.

Mac opened a sleepy eye. Spotting Sam and Amelia, he bounded off the sofa to give them a lick.

"He's going to be brilliant as Toto," said Amelia.

"I know." Sam grinned. "Come on – let's go and practise our parts!"

After dinner, Amelia finished her maths homework then went upstairs to learn her lines. Star was curled up on her bed. Amelia sat down beside her kitten and stroked her soft patchwork of ginger, brown and white fur. Star purred contentedly.

"Guess what, Star? I'm going to be Dorothy in *The Wizard of Oz!*"

The fact that she was going to be the

play's star still hadn't really sunk in.

Amelia changed into her pyjamas
and flopped down on the bed next to
Star. Then she read the whole play from
beginning to end.

"Dorothy's in every single scene!"

Amelia told Star. "There are so many lines to remember!"

Amelia read the scene that Miss Sachs had given them to learn over and over again. She said her lines out loud until her eyelids began to droop. The words began to swirl in her head. *Follow the yellow brick road … Follow the yellow brick road … Follow the …*

"Amelia? Are you awake?"

Amelia blinked. Her mum's voice was calling from behind the bedroom door. Amelia sat up and saw that the morning sun was streaming through her window, and the playscript was on the bed next to her. The clock said 07:03.

Oh no! I mustn't be late for Animal Ark!

"I'm up, Mum!" Amelia called. She pulled on her school uniform and rushed downstairs, where Gran made her some toast and poured her a glass of juice. She saw her gran's gym bag on a chair, her goggles balanced on top.

"Are you going swimming, Gran?" she asked.

"Aqua-aerobics, actually," said Gran. "We do keep-fit exercises in the swimming pool. The water supports your body so you don't put too much stress on your bones. It's the perfect exercise for my dodgy knee."

"That's interesting …" said Amelia.
Gran had just given her an idea for how
she might be able to help Oscar!

Amelia couldn't stop thinking about
aqua-aerobics as she walked through

the village to Animal Ark. Sam was already waiting at the entrance when she arrived.

"Learned your lines?" he asked.

"Sort of," said Amelia, trying to ignore the twinge of worry in her tummy. She probably needed to look at the script again, but there wasn't time now.

They got right down to work, cleaning out the pens in the hotel while Mr Hope checked the occupants. The tortoise had gone home, but Hoppy the rabbit was still there, as well as the parrot. "What a naughty boy!" it said, as Sam cleaned out its cage.

"No he's not," said Amelia, giggling.

There were some new animals in the hotel, too: a lizard who had gone off his food, three tiny baby gerbils and a large grey cat with an ear infection who was wearing a cone to stop her scratching.

When they'd finished in the overnight room, they were surprised to find Mrs Hope in reception with Miss Sachs and Oscar.

"He seems to be afraid to walk," Miss Sachs said, her eyes full of worry.

"I'd have expected Oscar to be putting

weight on his paw by now," said Mrs
Hope. "I'll take an X-ray to make sure
the break has mended. Come on, you
two," she said to Amelia and Sam.

Amelia grinned. *Mrs Hope is treating us
almost like real vets!*

In the X-ray room, Amelia watched
carefully as Mrs Hope laid the dog on
the table in the correct position. Then
she ushered them out of the room so she
could take the X-ray safely.

Afterwards, they looked at the X-ray
on the computer screen in Mrs Hope's
office. The bones in Oscar's leg showed up
bright white against a black background.

Mrs Hope examined the image. "The

break has healed perfectly," she told Miss Sachs. "Oscar just needs more time to get his strength back."

Amelia leaned over to stroke the little dog, who was sitting on Miss Sachs's lap. He looked back at her with sad eyes.

"Do you think aqua-aerobics would help Oscar's leg to recover?" Amelia asked. "My gran has a bad knee, and

she says that it really helps."

Mrs Hope's eyebrows rose. "It's possible, but the nearest hydrotherapy clinic for animals is in York. I'm afraid it's very expensive."

"I doubt I can afford it." Miss Sachs sighed and ruffled the dog's ears. "Oscar used to be so playful. I hate to see him like this."

Amelia saw tears in her drama teacher's eyes. She really wanted to help.

"It was worth a try," Sam whispered.

Amelia leaned over to give the dog another stroke. *I'll find a way to help you, Oscar. I don't know how, but I will!*

CHAPTER FOUR

After school, Amelia went to drama club. *I'm so tired*, she thought, stifling a yawn. She'd made a silly mistake in maths and couldn't seem to find the energy for football in PE. But she was determined to keep helping at Animal Ark before school and going to play rehearsals after. *I love both of them too much to stop!*

As she entered the school hall she saw Miss Sachs at the front, talking to a man with two wheelie suitcases. Oscar lay under a chair, his furry head resting on his paws.

"Hello everyone!" Miss Sachs said once the rest of the cast had arrived. "This is Caleb's dad, Mr Parish. He's a clothes designer and he's kindly offered to make our costumes for the play."

Caleb's father

smiled. "All right, thespians!" he said.
"Can you please line up and tell
me your names and the part you're
playing?"

The actors formed an orderly queue.

"What's a thespian?" Sam asked
Amelia.

"It's a posh word for 'actor'," said
Karel, behind them.

After everyone had told Mr Parish
which character they were playing, he
unzipped his suitcases and took out the
various costumes. "Don't worry if they
aren't the right size," he told the children
as he handed them out. "I'll be altering
them to fit."

"Ew! This is horrible!" Tiffany held up a black cloak and a pointy black hat. "I want glitter and sequins. Like that!" She pointed to Izzy's costume.

"But Izzy is the Good Witch," Mr Parish pointed out. "And you're the Wicked Witch."

"Well, I'm not wearing this costume," Tiffany complained.

"Why don't you try it on and then see what you think, Tiffany?" Miss Sachs suggested.

Sam was so delighted with his scarecrow costume that he tried it on over his uniform. "I love it!"

Amelia grinned at Sam's denim dungarees and patchwork shirt. There were bits of straw poking out of the collar and sleeves. "We can put you in the field at Spring Farm to scare away the crows!" she joked.

Mr Parish gave Amelia a blue checked dress with puffy sleeves. "Here's

Dorothy's costume. I'm still looking for a pair of ruby slippers for you to wear."

"Thank you, Mr Parish!" Amelia ran to the girls' toilets to change. She looked at herself in the mirror and smiled. With her hair in plaits, the costume would look even better. *Maybe I can make some ruby slippers myself,* she thought as she headed back to the hall humming

Follow the Yellow Brick Road.

"Hey, Dorothy!" Caleb the Cowardly Lion waved to Amelia as she came in. He wore a long fake fur coat with a shaggy mane around his face. All he needed now was lion face paint. Nearby, Amelia spotted Karel in his Tin Man costume made of shiny silver fabric. The characters from *The Wizard of Oz*

were starting to come alive!

The school hall buzzed with excitement as Mr Parish and Miss Sachs checked the fit of the costumes and made adjustments. Even Tiffany was dressed in her Wicked Witch costume, practising her cackle.

Only Oscar wasn't joining in with the excitement. The little dog still lay under the chair. *I wish I had more free time to play with you*, Amelia thought, going over to pat Oscar.

"Hey Amelia, look at my hat!"

Amelia looked up and laughed. A straw hat covered Sam's curly black hair, bits of hay poking out from underneath.

"How's Oscar?" asked Sam.

"He still seems so sad," said Amelia. "And he's not moving around. What can we do to cheer him up?"

"I know." Sam rummaged in his schoolbag and pulled out a rubber bone. "He can have this – I carry it around for Mac."

Amelia held the bone out for Oscar to sniff. He slowly clambered out from under the chair on his three good legs,

keeping his weak leg raised.

"Oscar, fetch." Amelia tossed the bone towards Sam. Oscar hobbled over to get it and brought it back to Amelia.

"Well done!" she said, rubbing his soft ears.

They played fetch while the others had their costumes adjusted. After a while, Miss Sachs came over. "Thank you so much for entertaining Oscar," she said.

"Miss Sachs, I've been thinking," said Amelia. "Maybe you could try hydrotherapy for Oscar in your bath at home?"

Miss Sachs sighed. "I wish I could, but my flat only has a shower."

"Your dog's really cute, Miss Sachs," asked Caleb, coming over to stroke Oscar. "Dad says we can get a pet, but we're not sure what kind to get."

"Dogs are great," said Sam. "But they're a lot of work."

"My parents are both pretty busy," said Caleb.

As if on cue, Mr Parish came over to check Amelia's costume. He pinned the waist, where it was a bit loose.

"How about a cat?" Amelia suggested to Caleb. "You don't need to walk them, like dogs."

Caleb shook his head. "Mum's allergic to cats."

"Maybe a gerbil?" said Sam. "They don't take up much space."

Caleb shook his head and the fluffy hood with his Cowardly Lion mane fell back.

"Gerbils are boring," he said. "I want an interesting pet."

"We've got lots of land around the farmhouse," said Mr Parish, putting Caleb's hood back on his head again. "So space isn't a problem."

Miss Sachs clapped her hands for attention. "Listen, everyone! Now that you all look the part, let's give this scene a try, shall we?"

Still wearing their costumes, the cast

gathered together and formed a circle.

"All right, Amelia," said Miss Sachs.
"Take it away!"

Everyone turned to face Amelia. She
opened her mouth – but froze under
their expectant stares. Her mind went
completely blank.

"Toto, where are we?" prompted Tiffany. She rolled her eyes. "Don't you even know the first line?"

Amelia managed to remember the next few lines with only a few stumbles. But when Dorothy met Glinda the Good Witch, Amelia looked at her friend and accidentally called her Izzy.

"I'm Glinda," Izzy whispered.

"Sorry, Izzy," said Amelia. "I mean Glinda …"

Suddenly, Tiffany stepped forward, swirling her black cape dramatically. "Hee-hee-hee!" she cackled loudly.

Amelia was so surprised she couldn't remember what to do next. "I'm sorry, Miss Sachs," she said, fighting to hold back her tears. "I thought I'd learnt my lines by heart, but I keep forgetting them."

"It's only our first rehearsal," said Miss Sachs. "Don't worry, Amelia. Why not read from the script if you can't quite remember the words?"

Tiffany scowled and waved her witch's wand at Amelia. "She'll ruin our play if she can't memorise her part."

"Give Amelia a chance," said Sam loyally.

"Yeah, why don't you come over to

my house tomorrow after school?" said Caleb. "We can run through the scene a few times, and talk about pets too!"

Amelia did her best to smile. But as she picked up her script, she was worried that Tiffany might be right ...

CHAPTER FIVE

"Here we are," said Mr Parish, as he turned the car into a long driveway the following day after school. The late afternoon sunshine lit up the fields on either side of the drive.

In the back seat of the car, Amelia yawned. She felt more like taking a nap than rehearsing. *But I need to learn my lines*, she thought with a flutter of worry. She really didn't want to mess up again.

Next to her, Mac sat on Sam's lap, yapping cheerfully as the car approached a large farmhouse at the end of the drive. As soon as the car stopped, Caleb jumped out. "Come on," he said. "I'll show you around!"

While Mr Parish went inside, Amelia, Sam and Mac followed Caleb to an enormous old barn behind the farmhouse. Caleb swung open the door and Amelia saw that the barn was empty. Mac kicked up sawdust and scraps of hay from the floor as he scampered from one end to the other.

"Mac, heel," called Sam. The little puppy ran back to his side. "Good boy."

"He's so cool," said Caleb, with a sigh. "I can't wait to have a pet of my own."

"You've definitely got the space for it!" said Sam, gazing around. "This place is huge."

"We might turn it into a farm shop," said Caleb. "Mum wants to sell food grown by farmers all around Welford. It's so different living here! We used to live in a flat in London."

"You'll get used to the countryside in no time," said Amelia.

Caleb led them into what Amelia guessed must once have been a stable. Unlike the empty barn, it was packed. A pin board was attached to one wall, with photographs and drawings of outfits. A table was covered in sketches, and there were shelves stacked with fabrics in all different colours and patterns. Amelia recognised the blue checked fabric of her

Dorothy costume. There were cotton reels in a rainbow of colours and boxes filled with buttons and zips. By the window, there was even a pair of dummies wearing brightly coloured shirts, pinned in place.

"This is Dad's studio," said Caleb proudly.

"Wow!" said Amelia. She turned to the others, feeling a little shy. "Should we practise that scene now? I did so badly at rehearsal yesterday—"

"Of course!" said Caleb.

"Don't be so hard on yourself," said Sam. "You've got the most lines. But we'll help you remember them!"

Amelia grinned, feeling happier already.

They marked out an area of the barn to use as a makeshift stage. Since the Scarecrow and the Cowardly Lion weren't in the first scene, Sam played Glinda and Caleb was the Wicked Witch of the West.

Amelia spun around and around with Mac in her arms, pretending she was being whirled about by a tornado. "Toto, where are we?"

This time, without so many people watching, the rehearsal went much better. Amelia remembered nearly all her lines. When they finished their run-through, the sound of applause echoed from the doorway of the barn. Amelia glanced over and saw a woman with long curly hair clapping.

"Mum!" said Caleb. "How long were you watching?"

"Oh, not very long," said Mrs Parish. "Come on in now. Dinner's ready."

They all sat round a big pine table and ate a delicious dinner of lasagne with apple crumble for pudding. After dinner, Amelia, Sam and Caleb played football in one of the big fields outside, while Mac chased the ball.

By now, the sun was a fiery orange ball

setting over the fields. When their game was over, they piled into the car so Mr Parish could drive them home.

But on the way, the car started juddering and making an odd noise.

Wap! Wap! Wap!

"Oh no! We must have a flat tyre," said Mr Parish.

He stopped the car in a lay-by next to a pasture and got out to check. The children and Mac stayed in the car.

"Look, Sam, there's your twin!" said Caleb, pointing out of the window.

"Huh? I haven't got a— Oh!" Sam started laughing.

In the middle of the field stood a

scarecrow, wearing ragged old trousers
and a faded red checked shirt.

Amelia spotted two animals grazing
in the pasture behind the scarecrow.
They were white and woolly like sheep,
but much bigger and with long necks.

"Those must be Mr Nicholls' llamas,"

she said. "The ones who need a new home."

"Here he comes!" said Sam.

Mr Nicholls was ambling towards the car, with his black and white sheepdog at his heels.

"How's Lucy?" Amelia called through the open window.

Farmer Nicholls stopped and smiled. "Much better since Mr Hope took out that sore tooth!" He turned to Mr Parish. "Can I help?"

"I've got a flat tyre," said Mr Parish. "But I left the jack at home."

"My tractor has a forklift attachment that should do the job," Farmer Nicholls offered. "Why don't you kids go and say hi to Llarry and Lliam over there, while we fix the tyre? They'll eat grass out of your hand if you feed them."

"Whoa!" said Caleb. "I've never met a llama before."

"Me neither," said Amelia, grinning. "Let's do it!"

CHAPTER SIX

A breeze rippled across the field as
Amelia, Sam and Caleb climbed out of
the car and walked through the gate
to the pasture. Mac came with them
on his lead. Curious, the llamas walked
over to them, heads bobbing.

Amelia reached out to pet Llarry, the

bigger one. His shaggy white wool was
thick and soft. Sam picked a handful
of grass and held it out, then Caleb did
the same. The llama chewed it slowly,
gazing at them with big brown eyes
surrounded by long lashes.

Meanwhile, in the fading light,
Amelia saw the farmer's tractor rumble

down the lane. A moment later, the front of the car rose up in the air.

Caleb fed more grass to Lliam, the smaller llama, and stroked his nose. "These llamas are so friendly. They're totally amazing!" His eyes were almost as wide as the llama's, and a big grin was plastered on his face.

"Mac isn't sure about them," laughed Sam. "Look!"

The little Westie puppy was sniffing the llamas, but not getting too close.

By the time the tyre was fixed, the moon and stars glowed in the dark sky. But Caleb didn't want to leave the llamas when his dad and Mr Nicholls came over to fetch them.

Amelia had an idea.

"Mr Nicholls can't keep Llarry and Lliam any more because he's moving house. Maybe you could adopt them?" she suggested.

"They could live in the fields outside your farmhouse," Sam pointed out.

"And they definitely aren't boring," added Amelia.

Caleb's eyes lit up. "Oh yes, please Dad! Llamas would be the perfect pets."

Mr Parish stroked the smaller llama and smiled. "Hmm, that's not a bad idea. Maybe I could use their wool to make clothes with …"

"They're brilliant pets," said Mr Nicholls, "although they can be a bit naughty sometimes."

As if to prove his point, the bigger llama plucked off the farmer's hat with his teeth.

Back at home, Amelia was in a chatty mood as she got ready for bed. She'd felt so tired earlier on, but after the excitement of the day she was wide awake.

"I hope the Parishes decide to adopt the llamas," she told Mum and Gran. She was standing on the landing, her toothbrush in one hand. "Oh, and I've had an idea about Oscar, too!"

"Who's Oscar?" asked Mum. "Is he in your class?"

Amelia laughed. "He's Miss Sachs's dog. You know, the one who had a broken leg. Mrs Hope said that hydrotherapy might help Oscar's leg get stronger, but Miss Sachs only has a shower at her flat. So I was wondering..." Amelia paused to let Gran get past on the landing. "I thought maybe we could do exercises with Oscar in our bath."

"Like aqua-aerobics for dogs?" asked Gran.

"Exactly!" Amelia smiled.

"Are you sure that's a good idea?" asked Gran, frowning.

"I'll phone Animal Ark in the morning and talk to the Hopes about it," said Mum.

Amelia grinned. "Thanks, Mum!" She brushed her teeth, put on her pyjamas and snuggled up in bed with Star purring softly at her feet. Turning out the light, she closed her eyes. Her mind raced with thoughts – about the play, about the llamas and about Oscar. She wondered what the Hopes would say about her idea.

They've GOT to say yes, she thought as her eyes closed.

"I think it's a brilliant idea!" said Mrs Hope the next morning, after Amelia had explained her hydrotherapy plan.

"Good thinking, Amelia!"

Amelia grinned. She couldn't wait to tell Miss Sachs her idea.

"Just be careful not to overdo it," said Mr Hope. "Short bursts only."

Amelia was still buzzing after school.

"Are you sure your mum and gran don't mind?" asked Miss Sachs, when Amelia told her before rehearsal.

"I'm positive," said Amelia. "Should we start after rehearsal?"

"That would be brilliant if it's not too much trouble," said Miss Sachs.

The rehearsal went really well. The extra practice with Sam, Caleb and Mac had paid off.

"You're not a bad Dorothy, I suppose," Tiffany admitted.

After rehearsal, Miss Sachs and Oscar came home with Amelia. Miss Sachs had a cup of tea with Gran, while Amelia prepared a warm bath for the little dog.

"Ready!" called Amelia.

Star ran into the bathroom and leapt on to the windowsill where she usually sat to keep Amelia company in the bath. But when Miss Sachs brought Oscar upstairs to the bathroom, the kitten's tail puffed up with fear.

"Don't worry, Star," Amelia told her. "Oscar won't hurt you."

The little kitten watched suspiciously

from the windowsill, her spine arched.
Amelia carefully lifted Oscar around his
furry brown tummy and gently started
to lower him into the warm bath.

   I really hope this works, thought Amelia.
Would Oscar sink or swim?

CHAPTER SEVEN

Oscar whimpered and squirmed as his legs touched the bath water.

"I'm not sure he likes it," said Miss Sachs worriedly.

But as Amelia lowered Oscar further, he started to paddle. Amelia sighed with relief as his paws churned up the water.

"Well done, Oscar!" praised Amelia.

"He's even moving his bad leg a bit," Miss Sachs observed.

"Go, Oscar, go!" Amelia encouraged the little dog.

She held Oscar gently, letting him paddle some more. After a few minutes, he slowed down and started panting, so Amelia lifted him out of the bath.

"The towel on the rail is for Oscar," she said to Miss Sachs.

But as the drama teacher reached for the towel, Oscar squirmed out of Amelia's arms and shook himself, spraying water everywhere! Star meowed loudly and darted out the door.

Amelia and Miss Sachs laughed as they dried their faces.

"You little scamp!" Miss Sachs scooped Oscar up from the floor and ruffled his fur with the towel. "Now, let's see how that leg is doing," she said, as she set him down on the bathroom floor.

But Oscar still stood on only three legs, lifting the other one off the floor. Amelia sighed with disappointment.

"He's not holding it as high as before,"

Miss Sachs pointed out. "It will just take time to get back to normal, like Mrs Hope said."

Amelia nodded. "You're right," she said. "I guess we'll just have to keep practising – just like we're doing for the play!"

The next day was Saturday. Amelia and Sam knew the routine at Animal Ark now. First they cleaned the pens in the overnight room and restocked the shelves with new food and toys. Then they helped with the day's patients.

Today, there was a large St Bernard

dog with an
upset tummy,
a guinea pig

with a skin allergy and a tabby cat who
was going to be spayed so she wouldn't
have kittens.

At eleven o'clock, Mr Nicholls came
in with Lucy.

"Are Lucy's teeth bothering her
again?" asked Amelia.

"She's fine," said the farmer. "I've just
come in to buy some chew sticks. By
the way, your friend Caleb is going to
have two new pets soon."

"The llamas?" said Amelia and Sam
together, excitedly.

Mr Nicholls laughed. "That's right. They'll be moving to the Parishes' house next week. Thanks for helping me find a good home for them."

Amelia's grin spread from ear to ear. Caleb wasn't going to have one cool new pet – he was going to have two!

On Sunday, Amelia made the ruby slippers for her Dorothy costume. She put a pair of old trainers Mac had chewed on some newspaper in the garden. Mum brushed PVA glue all over the shoes, then Amelia sprinkled lots of red glitter on them.

Star wanted to help too, but Amelia waved the kitten away.

"I'm sorry, Star, but I don't want you to turn into a ruby kitten!" she said.

While her shoes were drying, Miss Sachs brought Oscar over for another hydrotherapy session. This time, the little terrier didn't hesitate to get into the bath, with Amelia holding him firmly around the middle. As soon as she lowered him into the water, he started paddling with all four legs.

"I think Oscar likes his hydrotherapy!" said Miss Sachs. "And it seems to be helping."

Sure enough, after they'd finished and dried the dog off, Oscar rested his bad paw on the floor.

"Hurray!" cheered Miss Sachs.

Her shout startled the dog, who scuttled across the floor to her. He lifted his leg up again.

"Oh," said Amelia, disappointed.

Miss Sachs smiled and rubbed Oscar's

ears. "He's getting there," she said. "And it's all thanks to you."

Amelia blushed. Oscar set down his paw again for a few seconds, before lifting it. He strained his neck towards the bath.

"I think he wants another go," said Miss Sachs.

As soon as Amelia lifted him up again, Oscar's tail began to wag. The moment she lowered him into the bath, his feet began to paddle.

I can't believe it's really working! thought Amelia.

"Go, Oscar!" she cried as the tiny terrier paddled in the bath.

Amelia was so busy that the next few weeks went by in a cheerful blur. What with school, rehearsing *The Wizard of Oz*, helping at Animal Ark, plus Oscar's hydrotherapy sessions, she barely had time to think.

On the day before the play, the drama club met in the school hall for a dress rehearsal. The cast all stood together on the stage.

Oscar sat at Miss Sachs's feet looking alert, all four paws firmly on the ground. Amelia smiled as she thought back to when she'd first met him at Animal Ark, wrapped up in a blanket. *He's like a different dog now!*

The cast all wore their costumes. Amelia's blue check dress fit perfectly now and her hair was in two plaits. Sam's dungarees and patchwork shirt, with straw sticking out everywhere, made him look like a real scarecrow. Even Mac wore a red neckerchief for his role as Toto.

"We're going to run through the entire play," called Miss Sachs from

the floor. "Places, everyone!"

Everyone hurried off the stage. The stage curtain closed and then it opened again, signalling the start of the play. Amelia hugged Mac and spun around as if she was being whirled in a tornado.

"Toto, where are we?" she began.

The rehearsal went smoothly until the play's finale. Dorothy and Toto were running away from the Wicked Witch's castle with the Scarecrow, the Tin Man and the Cowardly Lion.

"You'll never escape from me!" cackled Tiffany as the Wicked Witch.

"Oh yes we will," replied Amelia.

She grabbed the pail of water from the side of the stage and threw it on the Wicked Witch. But Tiffany jumped out of the way and the water splashed all over Mac instead! The little Westie whimpered and shook himself dry, spraying water all over the Scarecrow, the Tin Man and the Cowardly Lion.

"I'm sorry, Mac!" gasped Amelia.

"Tiffany," said Miss Sachs, "Dorothy is supposed to throw the water at the Wicked Witch."

"And then the Wicked Witch melts away," added Sam, wiping drops of water off his face with his sleeve.

"But I don't want to get all wet," Tiffany protested. "I'm a serious actress."

"As a serious actress, you should do what your director tells you," Miss Sachs said firmly. "Let's press on to the end."

Luckily they managed to get to the end without any more mishaps. Tiffany did her melting scene dry, but it was still very good.

"Well done, everyone," called Miss Sachs. "You've all worked so hard these past few weeks. Be sure to get a good night's rest! Tomorrow's the big day!"

CHAPTER EIGHT

At school the next day, every lesson
seemed to drag. Amelia couldn't
concentrate on her work at all. She
kept thinking of all the things that
might go wrong with the play – the
curtain falling down, someone slipping
in a puddle of water, and most of all,

the crowd booing when she forgot her lines …

That night, as Mum and Gran drove Amelia the short distance back to school, the ball of nerves in the pit of her stomach made her feel queasy. Her legs felt like jelly as she climbed out of the car. *What if I ruin the show?* Amelia thought.

Mum kissed the top of her head. "You know, I thought you'd taken on too many activities, what with Animal Ark and the play. But you've handled everything amazingly well and I know you're going to be great."

"Thanks, Mum," Amelia said, wishing

she shared her
mother's confidence.

"Break a leg," said
Gran, hugging her.
"That's what actors
say for good luck."

Despite their
encouragement,
Amelia couldn't
shake her jitters. She
paced up and down the hall, going over
her lines for what felt like the millionth
time.

I'm going to mess it up, she fretted,
wondering if she should just tell Miss
Sachs that she couldn't go on. That

would be better than getting on stage and freezing, letting everyone down …

Just then, Miss Sachs appeared in the doorway of the school hall. "Time to go backstage, everyone!"

As Amelia hurried into the dressing room with the rest of the cast, Oscar bounded up to her, tail wagging. *Maybe you're my lucky charm,* she thought hopefully. Dodging his friendly licks, she put Oscar in her basket and took him back to Miss Sachs.

When it was show time, Amelia waited on stage with Mac for the curtain to open. She could hear the murmuring of the audience on the other side, waiting for the play to start. She took a deep breath to steady herself. In her arms, Mac squirmed, his pointy white ears twitching.

"Are you nervous too, Mac?" she whispered.

As the music started – accompanied by a crash of thunder and howling wind – Mac began to bark loudly.

"Hush," said Amelia, trying to soothe him. "Remember, you're Toto and I'm Dorothy."

Suddenly, with a panicked wriggle, Mac squirmed out of her arms.

"Mac! Come back!" called Amelia in a low voice.

But he wasn't paying attention at all. She saw Sam try to catch him at the side of the stage, but Mac hid behind the brightly painted scenery of the Land of Oz.

"What are we going to do?" cried Sam. "Mac won't come out."

"He's got stage fright," declared Tiffany. "I knew Sparkle should've got the part of Toto."

"He probably doesn't want to get splashed again," said Sam indignantly.

Miss Sachs slipped through the gap in the curtain. "I'm sorry for the delay," Amelia heard her announce to the audience. "The show will begin as soon as possible."

Amelia knelt down by the scenery where Mac was hiding. "Come on out, Mac. Please!"

"Mac, heel!" Sam ordered. "Come!"

But Mac wouldn't budge. His ears were flattened and he was trembling.

Just then, Oscar bounded up to Amelia, and sat neatly at her feet.

"Oscar, what are you doing on stage?" whispered Amelia.

The little terrier looked at her with his big brown eyes and wagged his tail.

Suddenly, Amelia smiled. "Oscar, do  you want to be Toto?"

He wagged his tail some more.

Amelia picked him up. He licked her cheek with his pink tongue. "Miss

Sachs, I think we've got a new Toto!"

Miss Sachs gave a smile of relief.
"Phew! Thank goodness we have an
understudy." She turned to the cast.
"Places, everyone! It's show time!"

Amelia hurried to the centre of the
stage with Oscar. A moment later, the
curtain opened.

Amelia looked out at the faces in the
audience. She saw Mum and Gran in
the front row, Mr and Mrs Hope, Mr
Nicholls, the Parishes, Mr Ferguson
and lots of other people that she'd met
in the village since she'd moved here.
Sam's parents were there, with Mac
now sitting calmly on Mrs Baxter's lap.

He looked much happier now that he wasn't on stage.

Amelia swallowed hard. Her heart was thumping. She looked down at Oscar.

If you're brave enough to get over your broken leg, then I'm brave enough to get over a bit of stage fright.

She took a deep breath and spun around with Oscar in her arms.

"Toto, where are we?" she said, her voice loud and clear.

As the play went on, Amelia felt like she really was Dorothy. Oscar made a brilliant Toto, too. He didn't wriggle when Amelia held him and he wagged his tail on cue. Everyone remembered their lines, and Tiffany was truly terrifying as the Wicked Witch!

"You'll never escape from me, Dorothy! Hee-hee-hee!" she cackled, her face painted bright green under her black witch's hat.

"Oh yes I will," Amelia declared.

SPLASH! She threw the pail of water over her classmate.

Tiffany gave a dramatic shriek and pretended to shrivel up into a ball.

At the end of the show, the entire cast came back on stage to take their bows as the audience clapped loudly. Amelia stood in the middle with Sam on one side and Caleb on the other. She looked out at Mum and Gran, smiling and clapping in the front row.

We did it! she thought, glowing with pride.

As the cast took their final bow, Oscar bounded out on to the stage in front of them. That made the crowd applaud even more loudly. Amelia beamed as she saw how well the little dog's leg had healed.

Laughing, Amelia picked Oscar up and waved his paw at the audience. "I couldn't have done it without you," she whispered in his ear. "You were the real star of the show!"

The End

Turn the page for a sneak peek at
Amelia and Sam's next adventure!

ANIMAL ARK

Runaway Hamster

Lucy Daniels

Amelia knocked and pushed the door open. Lena and Sofia were scowling at each other. But when they saw Sam and Amelia, their faces broke into smiles. "Hi!" they said at the same time.

Amelia popped the lid off the tub, and held it out proudly. The twins stared into it. Lena wrinkled her nose. "Are they biscuits?"

"Hamster treats," Amelia said. "For Nibbles!"

The twins leapt up in delight. "Whoa! Thank you, that's amazing!" cried Lena.

"We thought they might get him to eat," explained Sam.

Amelia felt something nudge her foot.

She looked down and saw a clear plastic ball with a little golden hamster running inside, pushing the ball along. It bumped into a chair, and the hamster sat up and rubbed his paws. Then he turned around, and the ball rolled towards the door.

Amelia grinned. "It looks like Nibbles is feeling better! Shall we see what he thinks of the treats?"

"Oh, that's not Nibbles," said Sofia. "It's Nacho."

Amelia caught Sam's confused expression. "Nacho?" she asked. "Have you got two hamsters?"

"Yes," said Lena. "Nibbles is in his own ball – he went behind the sofa ..."

Amelia leaned over the sofa and saw the hamster ball, but it was empty. Its small door was hanging open.

"Er, guys – he's not in there," she said.

Both twins scrambled over to look.

"You must not have closed it properly," Lena accused her sister.

"I put Nacho in his!" said Sofia. "You did Nibbles."

"No I didn't!"

"It doesn't really matter," interrupted Sam.

The twins looked at each other. "We have to find him!" said Lena.

"OK, let's not panic," said Amelia, glancing around the floor. Hopefully

Nibbles hadn't gone far.

They searched under the armchairs and the sofa, but there was no sign of the hamster. Then Lena and Sofia checked the kitchen and the bathroom. When they came back into the living room, Lena's bottom lip began to quiver.

"Nothing," said Sofia, her eyes filled with tears.

"Don't worry," Amelia said quickly. "I'm sure we'll find him."

"Where's his cage?" asked Sam.

"In our bedroom," said Sofia. "It's on the next floor up, but Nibbles is good at climbing."

She led Amelia and Sam towards the

stairs, but Sofia said crossly, "Lena, you forgot Nacho. Don't you care if we lose him too?" She picked up the other hamster in his ball, pushed past Lena and stomped up the stairs.

Lena glowered. "Well, at least I shut Nacho's ball properly."

"No, that was *me*!"

"It doesn't matter whose fault it is," Amelia interrupted. "Poor Nibbles is lost and we need to find him."

The twins' bedroom was cramped and untidy. Bunk beds, one piled with a messy duvet and tangled pyjamas, the other neatly made, stood against one wall. One half of the floor was littered with toys and clothes, the other was spotless, with books arranged on a shelf and toys in a line. There was a hamster cage on the floor by the window. It wasn't very big and was crammed with climbing ramps, chewed cardboard tubes, a wheel, a litter tray and a food bowl. The bottom was lined with wood chippings and sawdust.

Lena checked inside and shook her head. "He's not in here."

Read **Runaway Hamster** to find out what happens next...

Animal Advice

Do you love animals as much as Amelia and Sam? Here are some tips on how to look after them from veterinary surgeon Sarah McGurk.

Caring for your pet

1. Animals need clean water at all times.
2. They need to be fed too – ask your vet what kind of food is best, and how much the animal needs.
3. Some animals, such as dogs, need exercise every day.
4. Animals also need lots of love. You should always be very gentle with your pets and be careful not to do anything that might hurt them.

When to go to the vet

Sometimes animals get ill. Like you, they will mostly get better on their own. But if your pet has hurt itself or seems very unwell, then a trip to the vet might be needed. Some pets also need to be vaccinated, to prevent them from getting dangerous diseases. Your vet can tell you what your pet needs.

Helping wildlife

1   Always ask an adult before you go near any animals you don't know.

2   If you find an animal or bird which is injured or can't move, it is best not to touch it.

3   If you are worried, you can phone an animal charity such as the RSPCA (SSPCA in Scotland) for help.

ANIMAL ARK

Where animals need you!

COLLECT ALL OF AMELIA AND SAM'S EXCITING ADVENTURES!

Kitten Rescue
Lucy Daniels

Bunny Trouble
Lucy Daniels

Fox Cub Danger
Lucy Daniels

Puppy in Peril
Lucy Daniels

The Purrfect Sleepover
Lucy Daniels

Doggy Drama
Lucy Daniels

Runaway Hamster
Lucy Daniels

Guinea Pig Superstar
Lucy Daniels
*Coming April 2019

The Lonely Pony
Lucy Daniels
*Coming April 2019

www.animalark.co.uk

🐾 Discover all the books in the series
🐾 Read exciting extracts
🐾 Find fun downloads
🐾 And lots more!